JUDY SIERRA, who holds a Ph.D. in folklore from the University of California,
is renowned in the USA for her funny and brief retellings of folktales.
She is devoted to storytelling and loves reading her books to children
in schools and libraries. She lives in California, USA.
This is her first book for Frances Lincoln.

MARC BROWN is best known as the creator of **Arthur the Aardvark**,
the star of many picture books and a five-time Emmy Award-winning
TV show. Marc has drawn upon his classical training at the
Cleveland Institute of Art to create colourful paintings for
Wild About Books that reflect the naïve spirit of folk art at its best.
He lives in Massachusetts, USA. This is his first book for Frances Lincoln.

Wild About Books

by JUDY SIERRA

pictures by MARC BROWN

F
FRANCES LINCOLN
CHILDREN'S BOOKS

It started the summer of 2002,
When the Springfield librarian, Molly McGrew,
By mistake drove her bookmobile into the zoo.
Molly opened the door and she let down the stair,
Turned on the computer and sat on her chair.

At first all the animals watched from a distance,
But Molly could conquer the strongest resistance.

By reading aloud from the good Dr. Seuss,
She quickly attracted a mink and a moose,
A wombat, an oryx, a lemur, a lynx,
Eight elephant calves and a family of skinks.

In a flash, every beast in the zoo was stampeding
To learn all about this new something called reading.

Forsaking their niches, their nests, and their nooks,
They went wild, simply wild, about wonderful books,
Choosing thin books and fat books and **Cat in the Hat** books
And new books and true books and heaps of how-to books.

Giraffes wanted tall books and crickets craved small books,
While geckos could only read stick-to-the-wall books.

The pandas demanded more books in Chinese.
Molly filled their requests, always eager to please.
She even found waterproof books for the otter,
Who never went swimming without **Harry Potter**.

Raccoons read alone and baboons read in bunches.

And llamas read dramas while eating their llunches.

Hyenas shared jokes with the red-bellied snakes,
And they howled and they hissed till their funny bones ached.

A tree kangaroo, who adored **Nancy Drew**,
Began solving mysteries right there at the zoo,
Such as, why were the bandicoot's books overdue?

Gently, Molly taught lessons in treating books right,
For the boa constrictor squeezed **Crictor** too tight,
Baby bunnies mucked up **Goodnight Moon** with their paws,
Giant termites devoured **The Wizard of Oz**,

And bears' love of books was completely outrageous –
They licked all the pictures right off all the pages.

BIG BAD
BRUCE

Tasmanian devils found books so exciting

That soon they had given up fighting for writing.

They made up adventures so thrilling and new

That the others decided to be authors, too.

Pythons wrote with their tails, penguins wrote with their bills,

And porcupines wrote with their very own quills.

INK

Mice are nice.

At the new insect zoo, bugs were scribbling haiku.
(The scorpion gave each a stinging review.)

Walking Stick

A cannibal twig
Silently devours a leaf—
Eating, not eaten.

Pretentious.

Dung Beetle

Roll a ball of dung—
Any kind of poo will do—
Baby beetle bed.

Stinks.

It was a dark
and stormy
night. The wind
howled. The moon
cast a mournful
pale yellow glow.
Dogs waited in
the st...

As the cheetah's new novel began to take shape,
He read chapters each night to the Barbary ape;
And although the gazelle couldn't spell very well,
Like everyone else, she had stories to tell.

Imagine the hippo's enormous surprise
When her memoir was given the Zoolitzer Prize.

With so many new books, Molly knew what to do –
She hired twelve beavers, a stork, and a gnu
To build a branch library there at the zoo.
Then the animals cried, "We can do it ourselves!
We can check the books out. We can put them on shelves."

And they did, and they do, up to this very day.
Three cheers for the Zoobrary—

Hip, hip, hooray!

When you visit the zoo now, you surely won't mind
If the animals seem just a bit hard to find –
They are snug in their niches, their nests, and their nooks,
Going wild, simply wild, about wonderful books.

Would you like to read any of the stories that
drove the animals simply wild about wonderful books?
Here are a few of the animals' favourites:

The Cat in the Hat by Dr. Seuss
Crictor by Tomi Ungerer
Goodnight Moon by Margaret Wise Brown
The Harry Potter series by J.K. Rowling
The Nancy Drew series by Carolyn Keene
The Wizard of Oz by L. Frank Baum

Text copyright © Judy Sierra 2004
Illustrations copyright © Marc Brown 2004. All Rights Reserved.
First published in the USA in 2004 by Alfred A. Knopf,
an imprint of Random House Children's Books.
Published by arrangement with Random House Children's Books,
a division of Random House, Inc. New York, USA. All Rights Reserved.

Published in Great Britain in 2006 by
Frances Lincoln Children's Books, 4 Torriano Mews,
Torriano Avenue, London NW5 2RZ

www.franceslincoln.com

First paperback edition 2007

British Library Cataloguing in Publication Data available on request

ISBN: 978-1-84507-612-2

Printed in China

3 5 7 9 8 6 4

This book is for our favourite doctor,
artist, poet, fun concocter:
Theodor Seuss Geisel, 1904–1991.

Judy Sierra and Marc Brown

MORE STORIES IN PAPERBACK FROM FRANCES LINCOLN CHILDREN'S BOOKS

The Library
Sarah Stewart
Illustrated by David Small

Elizabeth Brown loves to read books. But now that she has grown up, her collection is so big that her bookshelves are collapsing. Her front door has disappeared entirely. What in the world will she do?

"A funny, heart-warming story" School Library Journal

ISBN 978-1-84507-607-8

Dashing Dog
Margaret Mahy
Illustrated by Sarah Garland

Follow the chaotic antics of the dashing dog and his family in a mad, dizzy and joyful walk along the beach.

"Anything written by Margaret Mahy is always worth reading" The Guardian

ISBN 978-0-7112-1977-9

Down the Back of the Chair
Margaret Mahy
Illustrated by Polly Dunbar

When Dad loses his keys, toddler Mary suspects they are down the back of the chair. Join in the fun as the family find everything from a bandicoot and a bumble bee to a string of pearls and a lion with curls. But will it be enough to save the family from rack and ruin?

"This is a delight" Daily Mail

ISBN 978-1-84507-602-3

Frances Lincoln titles are available from all good bookshops.
You can also buy books and find out more about your favourite titles, authors and illustrators on our website: www.franceslincoln.com